MIAMI HEAT

BY TOM GLAVE

SportsZone

An Imprint of Abdo Publishing
abdobooks.com

abdobooks.com

Published by Abdo Publishing, a division of ABDO, PO Box 398166, Minneapolis, Minnesota 55439. Copyright © 2023 by Abdo Consulting Group, Inc. International copyrights reserved in all countries. No part of this book may be reproduced in any form without written permission from the publisher. SportsZone™ is a trademark and logo of Abdo Publishing.

Printed in China
052022
092022

THIS BOOK CONTAINS
RECYCLED MATERIALS

Cover Photo: Cliff Hawkins/Getty Images Sport/Getty Images
Interior Photos: Melinda Nagy/Shutterstock Images, 1; Mike Ehrmann/Getty Images Sport/Getty Images, 4; Greg Fiume/Getty Images Sport/Getty Images, 7; David J. Phillip/AP Images, 8; Wilfredo Lee/AP Images, 9; Kevin C. Cox/Getty Images Sport/Getty Images, 11; Alan Greth/AP Images, 12; Focus on Sport/Getty Images Sport/Getty Images, 15, 24, 31; Rick Bowner/AP Images, 17; Jay Drowns/Sporting News/Getty Images, 18; Lynne Sladky/AP Images, 20; Craig Mitchelldyer/AP Images, 23; Rhona Wise/AFP/Getty Images, 27; Winslow Townson/AP Images, 29; Sue Ogrocki/AP Images, 33; Allsport/Getty Images Sport/Getty Images, 34; Gregory Shamus/Getty Images Sport/Getty Images, 37; Mike Segar/Reuters Pool/AP Images, 39; Mark J. Terrill/AP Images, 41

Editor: Charlie Beattie
Series Designer: Joshua Olson

Library of Congress Control Number: 2021951680

Publisher's Cataloging-in-Publication Data

Names: Glave, Tom, author.
Title: Miami Heat / by Tom Glave
Description: Minneapolis, Minnesota : Abdo Publishing, 2023 | Series: Inside the NBA | Includes online resources and index.
Identifiers: ISBN 9781532198335 (lib. bdg.) | ISBN 9781098271985 (ebook)
Subjects: LCSH: Miami Heat (Basketball team)--Juvenile literature. | Basketball--Juvenile literature. | Professional sports--Juvenile literature. | Sports franchises--Juvenile literature.
Classification: DDC 796.32364--dc23

TABLE OF CONTENTS

CHAPTER ONE

A SHOT TO REPEAT

Time was winding down on the Miami Heat in Game 6 of the 2013 National Basketball Association (NBA) Finals. The Heat were the defending champions, and they were facing elimination at the hands of the San Antonio Spurs. Down 95–92, the Heat had one more shot to save their season.

Staff at American Airlines Arena in Miami started setting up yellow police tape. It was there to keep fans off the court while the Spurs accepted the Larry O'Brien Championship Trophy. A ring of security also began to line the court. The Spurs and Heat looked like they were playing in a cage.

Less than two minutes earlier, it looked as if Miami might force Game 7. But then Spurs star guard Tony Parker tied the score at 89–89 with a tough three-pointer over the outstretched arm of Miami's LeBron James. On the next possession, Parker stole the ball from Heat guard

In 2013 LeBron James (6) and the Miami Heat took on a San Antonio Spurs team that had won four NBA Finals in the previous 14 years.

Mario Chalmers. The Spurs guard then gave his team the lead with a spinning jumper in the lane.

Suddenly, the Heat were on the ropes. Even worse, they were having trouble holding on to the ball. Miami's next two possessions resulted in turnovers. At the other end, Spurs guard Manu Ginóbili stretched the lead to 94–89 with three free throws. The Spurs were less than 30 seconds away from a championship unless a hero for the Heat stepped up.

BATTLE OF THE BIG THREES

Both teams had plenty of potential heroes. It was an NBA Finals for the ages. The veteran Spurs were looking for their fifth championship since 1999. Center Tim Duncan had been a part of all four previous titles. Parker and Ginóbili had been clutch performers when San Antonio won in 2003, 2005, and 2007.

Miami had its own Big Three. Guard Dwyane Wade had played his entire career with the Heat. He led the team to its first NBA title in 2006. After the 2009–10 season, he was joined by two other superstars. Center Chris Bosh came over from the Toronto Raptors. And James, one of the most complete players in league history, left the Cleveland Cavaliers to join the Heat. After reaching the NBA Finals in their first season together, the new-look Heat won a title in their second year.

Their hopes for a repeat, however, rested on a great supporting player. Ray Allen had been in the NBA since 1996.

Miami's Big Three of Dwyane Wade, *left*, LeBron James, *center*, and Chris Bosh led the Heat to the Finals four times in four seasons together.

Over the course of his career with the Milwaukee Bucks, Seattle SuperSonics, and Boston Celtics, he'd been one of the league's best scorers. Allen had even won an NBA title with Boston in 2008. By 2013 he was 37 years old. But the sharpshooting guard signed with Miami to take one more shot at a second title.

THE NBA FINALS

The teams had met twice during the regular season. Miami won both games, but each was close. The NBA Finals brought

Wade averaged 19.6 points and 4.6 assists during the 2013 Finals.

more drama. The Spurs held on late to win 92–88 in Game 1. A late shot by Parker sealed the win. Miami grabbed Game 2 thanks to a 33–5 run that blew open a close game.

The Spurs answered by hitting a record 16 three-pointers in Game 3. They outscored Miami 35–14 in the fourth quarter of a 113–77 romp. Game 4 was tied at halftime before Miami's Big Three took over. James, Wade, and Bosh combined for 85 points as the Heat tied the series. The Spurs answered again and took Game 5 at home behind strong performances from Ginóbili and young forward Danny Green.

Game 6 was back in Miami. The Heat needed another response. But as the fourth quarter began, it looked as if the Heat were out of answers. They trailed by 10 points. Then James took over. He scored 10 points on a 17–7 Miami run, and his layup with 6:34 left tied the game 82–82. The teams then went back and forth until the final minute, when the Heat started to let the game slip away.

THE FRANTIC FINAL SECONDS

After Ginóbili's clutch free throws, the Heat needed a basket quickly. On their next possession, James hoisted a three-pointer from atop the key. It missed, but teammate Mike Miller picked up a tipped rebound and sent the ball back to James. The superstar didn't miss his next attempt. The Spurs lead was cut to 94–92 with 20 seconds left.

The yellow rope and security guards crowded the floor as Duncan tried to inbound the ball after a timeout. He got the ball to teammate Kawhi Leonard, and Miller quickly fouled him. Leonard's first free throw spun out of the rim. He hit the second free throw, however. San Antonio led 95–92.

Ray Allen, *left*, had scored just two points going into the final minute of Game 6.

THE SHOT

Miami raced up the court for one more chance. James came off a screen and caught a pass on the left wing. Another three-point attempt was off the mark. Miami still had a chance. Bosh ripped down the rebound in the middle of three Spurs. James and Chalmers were open on the three-point line. But Bosh also spotted Allen moving toward the corner. He sent a quick pass to the veteran shooter. Allen smoothly stepped backward as he caught the ball. The move took him behind the three-point line. In the same motion, he leaped high and fired a three-pointer over Parker's raised arm. The shot dropped through with 5.2 seconds showing on the clock. Allen had tied the game.

The fans erupted. Allen's reaction was more subdued. He offered a quick fist pump as he saw the ball go through the hoop.

The Spurs had one more chance to win it. Miami's fans stood as the opponents attempted to do just that. But Parker missed a running jumper as time ran out. It was on to overtime.

LeBron James's triple-double in Game 6 was one of 11 he has recorded in the NBA Finals. It was also his second of the series against San Antonio. James had 18 points, 18 rebounds, and 10 assists in Miami's Game 1 defeat.

Allen launches his famous three-pointer over San Antonio point guard Tony Parker.

The extra session was low scoring. With just a few seconds left and Miami leading 101–100, the Spurs' Boris Diaw fouled Allen. Allen strolled to the line and sank both free throws. The veteran had once again made sure there would be a Game 7.

"It was by far the best game that I've ever been a part of," said James, who finished with 32 points, 10 rebounds, and 11 assists.

Two days later James led all scorers with 37 points as the Heat won 95–88 in Game 7. The win clinched back-to-back titles for Miami. It also cemented the legacy of the team's Big Three. But it was all made possible thanks to the veteran Allen, who saved Miami and let the Heat fight another day.

SEIKALY
4
HEAT
11

THE HEAT IS ON

The city of Miami laid the foundation for a professional basketball team before the NBA ever made things official. Construction began on Miami Arena in August 1986. Local fans picked a name for the potential new team in a contest that October. Meanwhile, an ownership group of Basketball Hall of Famer Billy Cunningham, sports agent Lewis Schaffel, and Ted Arison, owner of the Carnival Cruise Lines, led the charge for the new team.

In April 1987, the NBA announced it would add three new cities to the league. Minneapolis, Minnesota, and Charlotte, North Carolina, seemed to be front-runners. Miami was also in the mix. But the city had competition inside Florida. Orlando was also bidding for a new team.

The NBA made a surprise announcement on April 22, 1987. All four cities would be added. The Miami and Charlotte teams

Rookie guard Sherman Douglas (11) goes around a screen set by center Rony Seikaly (4) during a Heat game in 1990.

would start play in 1988. Orlando and Minnesota were set to start a year later.

A SLOW START

Miami came out to an indoor fireworks show before its first game on November 5, 1988. After it ended, most of the fireworks belonged to the visiting Los Angeles Clippers. The Heat scored only 13 points in the first quarter of a 111–91 loss.

The defeat was the start of a downward trend. Of the 17 players who suited up for the Heat in their first year, 10 were rookies. The young team didn't win a game until December 14. That night's 89–88 win over the Clippers snapped a 17-game, season-opening losing streak. The young team mobbed head coach Ron Rothstein in celebration. Those moments were rare during the first season, as the Heat finished an NBA-worst 15–67.

By the time Miami made the playoffs in 1991–92, Rothstein had resigned. New head coach Kevin Loughery still had one of the league's youngest teams. But now he had more talent, led by third-year forward Glen Rice and guard Steve Smith, who made the All-Rookie team. The team finished 38–44.

Miami was the first of the four expansion teams to make the postseason. It wasn't a long trip. Superstar guard Michael Jordan and the Chicago Bulls swept the Heat in three games. Jordan closed the series with a 56-point game in Miami.

Although the Heat had been to the playoffs, they had yet to post a winning record. That changed two years later when they finished 42–40. That brought them back to the playoffs. This time they managed to win not just one game but two against the top-seeded Atlanta Hawks. However, Atlanta rebounded to win the next two of the best-of-five series, and Miami was out again.

Guard Steve Smith and the Heat struggled to win games in the early 1990s.

Rice continued to star for the Heat over the next two seasons. He even piled up a team-record 56 points in a win over Orlando on April 15, 1995. But Miami was going backward. By the time Rice had his big game, Loughery had been let go. But bigger changes were in store for the young Heat.

THE RILEY ERA

In February 1995, change came at the top. Arison's family bought out Schaffel and Cunningham's interests in the team. Micky Arison, Ted's son, was named team chairman. One of his first hires was an NBA legend. Pat Riley had been an NBA champion as a player and coach with the Los Angeles Lakers. He'd also led the New York Knicks on deep playoff runs in the early 1990s. Now Arison hired him to remake the Heat.

Riley was named team president and coach. He had full control over the roster. One of his first moves was trading away his best player. Rice was shipped to the Charlotte Hornets as part of a deal for All-Star center Alonzo Mourning. Another big deal brought in All-Star guard Tim Hardaway from the Golden State Warriors. The Heat finished with 42 wins and made the playoffs. Though they were swept again by the Bulls, the foundation was set.

Riley, Hardaway, and Mourning led the Heat to the playoffs in six straight seasons. That included a team-record 61 wins during the 1996–97 season and a trip to the Eastern Conference finals. Along the way, they developed their first rival— Riley's former team, the Knicks.

In the 1997 playoffs, the Knicks built a 3–1 lead over Miami in a second-round series. But a fight at the end of Game 5 led to several suspensions for Knicks players. Miami rallied

The Heat developed a fierce, physical rivalry with the New York Knicks during the late 1990s.

to win the series. However, the Heat eventually fell to the powerhouse Bulls in the next round.

The rivals met again next postseason. This time another fight and more suspensions helped New York win the deciding game, ending Miami's season. The Knicks also ended Miami's season each of the next two years.

A NEW STAR

The Heat's strong run came to a quick halt in the early 2000s. They missed the playoffs back-to-back years in 2002 and 2003. But the team's rebuild took a major leap the following summer. The Heat drafted guard Dwyane Wade as the number five pick in the 2003 NBA Draft.

"We feel like we have one of the best players in the draft, if not the best," Riley said afterward. Indeed, Wade would soon become the centerpiece of Miami's team.

The other change came on the bench. Riley decided in October of that year to stop coaching and simply run the team as president. He promoted assistant Stan Van Gundy to take over. The Heat started slowly before winning 17 of their final 21 games to make the 2004 playoffs.

Dwyane Wade, *left*, teamed up with Shaquille O'Neal to deliver Miami its first championship in 2006.

That postseason run ended in the second round. But in the summer of 2004, Riley made another big move. He brought in All-Star center Shaquille O'Neal in a trade with the Lakers. O'Neal combined with Wade to take Miami to the Eastern Conference finals.

Riley was determined to get Miami over the hump. The summer of 2005 saw the addition of several role players. Point guard Gary Payton signed with the team. Guard Jason Williams and forwards Antoine Walker and James Posey came to Miami in trades. Mourning, who had left the team in 2002 to fight a life-threatening kidney disease, also returned.

One last change occurred after the season began. Van Gundy resigned to spend more time with his family, and Riley returned to the bench. Under his coaching, the Heat took off in March and roared into the postseason. The winning didn't stop there. With Wade leading the way, Miami captured its first championship by defeating the Dallas Mavericks in six games.

Dwyane Wade, *left*, and LeBron James celebrate their first NBA title together after beating the Oklahoma City Thunder in 2012.

Miami's aging roster was not set up for a dynasty, however. Key players left during the next few years. Even with one of the best players in the NBA still on the roster in Wade, Miami sank to a 15–67 record just two years after winning the championship.

Riley moved back into the front office again. This time young assistant coach Erik Spoelstra took over. But Miami was about to get a boost from outside the organization.

THE BIG THREE ARRIVE

Two of the NBA's best players were free agents in the summer of 2010. Center Chris Bosh was leaving the Toronto Raptors. Forward LeBron James was headed out of Cleveland. Both players were going to be expensive. Luckily for the Heat, the team had plenty of cash to spend.

The team traded for Bosh on July 7. The next day, James set up a live television event to announce his new team. He picked the Heat as well. With Wade still in his prime, Miami suddenly had a superteam.

The trio, known as the "Big Three," brought big expectations. That pressure rose when the Heat did not win an NBA title in their first season together, losing in a surprise upset to Dallas in the Finals. But a season later they lived up to the billing by knocking off the Oklahoma City Thunder in five games to capture Miami's second title.

The team rose to new heights in 2012–13. The Heat won a team-record 66 games, including a 27-game win streak from February 3 to March 25. At the time it was the second-longest win streak in NBA history. But the historic season nearly came to a quick end in the NBA Finals. The San Antonio Spurs built a late lead in Game 6. Only Heat guard Ray Allen's dramatic game-tying three-point shot forced overtime. Miami won to even the series, then took Game 7 for a second straight championship.

Miami's Big Three made one more Finals run in 2013–14 but lost in five games to the Spurs. James then left to go back to Cleveland. Bosh's career ended in 2016 due to illness. Even Wade eventually left, joining the Bulls in 2016 before returning to Miami at the end of his career.

YOUNG STARS

It took the Heat several seasons to rebuild back to championship contention. Once again they acquired an All-Star by trading for guard Jimmy Butler in the summer of 2019. Butler joined a young roster featuring forwards Bam Adebayo and Duncan Robinson and rookie guards Tyler Herro and Kendrick Nunn.

The season was paused in March because of the COVID-19 pandemic. When play resumed in August, Miami won its first three playoff series, losing only three games in the process. That set up a Finals showdown against the Lakers, who were now led by James. Butler recorded two triple-doubles in the Finals. But the Lakers took the series in six games. Still, Miami was once again a contender, now with several young stars who fans hoped would keep the team strong for years to come.

Tyler Herro, *right*, averaged 16.0 points per game in the playoffs during Miami's run to the 2020 NBA Finals.

CHAPTER THREE

HEAT HEROES

Glen Rice drew attention for his scoring ability while still in college at the University of Michigan. During the 1989 national championship tournament, Rice went on a scoring spree. In six games, he totaled 184 points while leading Michigan to the national title. He hit nearly 60 percent of his shots and made 27 three-pointers during the tournament.

Rice carried that shooting ability straight into the NBA. The Heat made him the fourth pick in the 1989 draft. They also immediately made him a go-to scorer.

In six seasons with the Heat, Rice averaged more than 19 points per game. He made his biggest dent in the scoreboard in his final season with the team. Rice piled up a career-high 56 points against the Orlando Magic on April 15, 1995. He hit seven three-point shots in the game.

Glen Rice averaged 19.3 points per game during his six seasons with the Heat.

Rice's scoring ability wasn't enough to keep him in Miami. When he left, the player who came in exchange turned out to be the Heat's next big star. Team president Pat Riley's first big move for the Heat was bringing center Alonzo Mourning to Miami.

Mourning was the kind of center Riley wanted to build a team around. A tough scorer and even tougher defender, Mourning owns the team record with 1,625 career blocks. He was named the NBA's Defensive Player of the Year twice while playing for the Heat. He led the league in blocks both of those years.

Bringing in Mourning wasn't Riley's only big move during the 1995–96 season. A flurry of trades brought Tim Hardaway to Miami in February 1996. The point guard was a great leader. He was also a quick dribbler and great passer who paired nicely with Mourning. The All-Star pair helped Miami reach the playoffs in six straight years.

Mourning missed most of the 2000–01 season after being diagnosed with a rare kidney disease. He returned in time for the playoffs. The next several years of Mourning's career were disrupted by his battle with the illness. He even missed an entire year in 2002–03 to go through treatment. When he came back to the NBA, it was with the New Jersey Nets. But he returned to Miami healthy during the 2004–05 season and helped the team win the NBA title in 2006.

Alonzo Mourning was one of Miami's first stars when he joined the team in 1995. After leaving the team in 2002, he returned as a key role player for the Heat's 2006 championship team.

THE CHAMPS

In NBA history, few drafts have produced superstars like 2003. LeBron James went first overall. High-scoring forward Carmelo Anthony and powerful center Chris Bosh were both off the board by the time the Heat used the fifth pick. Miami went with guard Dwyane Wade out of Marquette University. In college he had built a reputation as both a tough scorer and defender.

A solid first season landed Wade on the All-Rookie team and established him as the heart of the Heat. It was the start of a Miami career that included 13 All-Star appearances and the 2008–09 scoring title.

However, Wade will mostly be remembered for his three championships in Miami. And it was the addition of Shaquille O'Neal in 2004 that helped Wade blossom into one of the NBA's best players and best winners.

Upon arrival, O'Neal promised a championship in Miami. The outspoken center already had three of them from his time with the Lakers. His powerful inside presence freed up Wade to become a star, and the result was the Heat's first championship after the 2005–06 season.

Adding Chris Bosh (1) and LeBron James (6) in 2010 turned the Heat into an instant NBA powerhouse.

THE DECISION

James was already the league's top player when he told the world he was moving to South Beach to play for the Heat. James was drafted by his hometown Cleveland Cavaliers out of high school. He became an immediate star, helping Cleveland get to the playoffs five times. However, the Cavaliers never had enough talent around James to win it all.

Chris Bosh was in a similar situation in Toronto. He was a regular All-Star for the Raptors, but the team rarely made the playoffs. After spending the first seven seasons of his career in Toronto, Bosh was looking for a new home.

Both stars joined forces with Wade in Miami during the summer of 2010. The Heat found success with James and Wade sharing the scoring load. Bosh was less of a scorer than in his previous time in Toronto but contributed a powerful inside presence.

While the Big Three provided most of the offense, Miami also had a group of experienced role players to fill out the roster. Forward Udonis Haslem went undrafted out of the University of Florida, but he caught on with the Heat in 2003. By the team's first championship in 2006, he was a key contributor. Haslem joined Wade on all three Miami title teams.

The Heat also had strong veteran outside shooters in guards Mike Miller and Ray Allen. Rugged forwards Shane Battier and Chris Anderson patrolled the lane. And point guard Mario Chalmers was a steady ball handler. The Heat's dynasty of the 2010s revolved around its superstars. But several lesser-known players helped carry the load.

BENCH BOSSES

Pat Riley was an NBA legend before he ever set foot in Miami. He won four NBA titles with the "Showtime" Los Angeles Lakers

Pat Riley coached the Heat from 1995 to 2003 and again from 2005 to 2008.

in the 1980s. He also made the Knicks a powerhouse in the early 1990s. Still, Riley took his career to new heights with the Heat. He built a contender in the late 1990s, then rebuilt the roster twice in the 2000s to create championship teams. He also coached the team to its first title in 2006. The 2021–22 season marked his twenty-seventh season in charge of the Heat.

The only coach with more Miami wins than Riley is a man he hired. Erik Spoelstra started as an assistant to Riley in 1997, when he was 27 years old. He was still only 38 when he took over as head coach for Riley before the 2008–09 season. In 2020–21 Spoelstra picked up his 600th win with the team. He had surpassed his mentor by 146 victories.

THE NEXT GENERATION

After the departure of the Big Three, Miami rebuilt through the draft. Forward Bam Adebayo was the fourteenth selection in the 2017 draft. Within two years the versatile big man was an All-Star.

"Bam is one of the most dynamic unique players in the league," Spoelstra said in 2021. "He's an absolute hybrid on both ends of the court."

Adebayo was a star at the University of Kentucky before the Heat drafted him. Miami grabbed another former Wildcat in the 2020 first round. Shooting guard Tyler Herro started only eight games his rookie year. But he averaged 13.5 points per game in helping the Heat to the NBA Finals.

Miami's new leader came to the Heat through a trade in 2019. Small forward Jimmy Butler's intensity and skill guided Miami on a stellar postseason run. His arrival helped build a new kind of "Big Three" for the Heat as they looked to the future.

Miami forward Bam Adebayo dunks against the Oklahoma City Thunder during a game in 2021.

HEAT
10

CHAPTER FOUR

HEAT HIGHLIGHTS

Miami team president and coach Pat Riley didn't waste any time turning over the Heat lineup. One of his first actions upon arriving in Miami in 1995 was to trade for Alonzo Mourning.

Riley made three more moves just before that season's trade deadline in late February. A total of 10 players were traded. Five new players, including Tim Hardaway, came back to the Heat. But one day later, most of those new players were still not in town, even though the Heat had a game that night. Miami could barely field a roster against the mighty Chicago Bulls.

Miami dressed just eight players against the soon-to-be NBA champions. One of them was newly acquired guard Tony Smith. Another guard, Rex Chapman, led the Heat to an upset. He had 39 points and hit nine of 10 three-pointers in a stunning win.

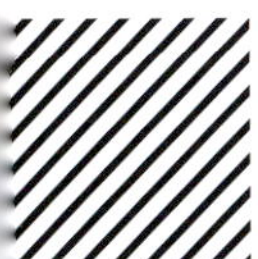

Picking up Tim Hardaway helped turn the Heat into a contender during the late 1990s.

By the start of the next season, Riley had all his pieces in place. He built a tough, defense-first mentality with the Heat. It paid off with a long road win streak. In November the team had to play six straight road games in a span of nine days. Miami won them all. In doing so, they picked up the nickname "Road Warriors." The name stuck all year long. Miami went 32–9 away from home during the 1996–97 season.

WONDERFUL WADE

Dwyane Wade earned his reputation as a big-game player in his first playoff game. Facing the New Orleans Hornets in the opening round of the 2004 playoffs, Wade's 10-foot jumper with 1.3 seconds left broke a 79–79 tie in a Miami win. It was just a taste of what was ahead.

Two years later Wade's star exploded in the 2006 NBA Finals. The series did not start well as Miami lost the first two games to the Dallas Mavericks. The Heat were behind again heading into the fourth quarter of Game 3. Dallas led 77–68. But Wade took over in the final 12 minutes. He scored 15 of his 42 points as Miami rallied to win 98–96.

The game turned the tide of the series. And Wade kept rolling. He added 36 points in a Miami rout over the Mavericks in Game 4. His Game 5 performance featured a pair of free throws with 1.9 seconds left in overtime that won the game 101–100. He finished the night with 43 points.

With Miami on the verge of a title in Game 6, Wade delivered again. His 36-point performance featured more late heroics. He scored Miami's final four points from the free-throw line in a 95–92 win. Dallas's Jason Terry missed a potential game-tying three-pointer in the final seconds. Wade grabbed the rebound. As the horn sounded, he flung the ball up in celebration. Wade was named the Finals Most Valuable Player (MVP) after averaging 34.7 points, 7.8 rebounds, and 3.8 assists in the series.

Dwyane Wade shoots over Detroit Pistons defender Chauncey Billups during the 2006 Eastern Conference finals.

Riley summed up what Wade meant to the Heat after the game. "He just took it to another level," Riley said. "Players like that are hard to come by. We're blessed to have him."

When Wade finally left the team for good in 2019, his name was all over the Heat record books. He was the team's all-time leader in games played, points, assists, and steals.

THE KING TAKES THE THRONE

The Big Three's first championship run wasn't always pretty. And that was especially true for LeBron James. The 6-foot-9-inch, 250-pound star forward had reached the NBA Finals once with the Cleveland Cavaliers before joining Miami. The San Antonio Spurs swept Cleveland while James shot just 35.6 percent.

In 2011 the Heat faced the Dallas Mavericks in the Finals. James averaged nearly nine fewer points in the series than he had in the regular season. Many around the NBA wondered if he had what it took to win.

James silenced those doubters the next year. After the Heat lost Game 1 to the Oklahoma City Thunder, James took over. He piled up 32 points in a 100–96 Game 2 victory. He followed that up with a 29-point, 14-rebound performance in a Game 3 victory.

Late in Game 4, James could barely move due to leg cramps. But he still had enough energy to break a 94–94 tie on a three-point shot with 2:51 left. Miami won 104–98. James finished one rebound shy of a triple-double.

Two days later James fully cemented his legacy. With a title on the line, he delivered the triple-double he had narrowly missed the game before. As the Heat climbed to a 121–106 victory, James finished with 26 points, 11 rebounds, and 13 assists. All three stats were team highs. Most importantly, he was finally a champion.

LeBron James flies for a dunk against the Oklahoma City Thunder during Game 5 of the 2012 NBA Finals.

RING THE BUTLER

Early in his career, Jimmy Butler earned a reputation for working hard and getting the most out of his talent. But he also became known as intense—sometimes too intense. When he joined the Heat in 2019, he was starting on his fourth team in four years. This time, though, everything clicked.

Miami finished with just the fifth-best record in the Eastern Conference. The Heat were not expected to make a deep playoff run. Due to the COVID-19 pandemic, all games were played in one location to keep the players isolated. The NBA chose Orlando, Florida, as its "bubble" for the playoffs. Butler turned the bubble into a home away from home. He was a force in the playoffs, averaging 22.2 points, 6.5 rebounds, and 6.0 assists. His play carried the Heat all the way to the NBA Finals. The team lost only three games in the first three rounds.

The championship series matched Miami up with the Los Angeles Lakers, now led by James. The experienced Lakers routed the Heat in the first two games. Miami needed an answer in Game 3. Butler had one, with a 40-point, 11-rebound, 13-assist performance. The Heat won 115–104.

Butler narrowly missed another triple-double in Game 4 as the Lakers won again. In Game 5, the Heat forward took over again. This time he finished with 35 points, 12 rebounds, and 11 assists. Miami survived to play another day with a 111–108 win.

After the game, Heat head coach Erik Spoelstra had high praise for his star. "Every young player coming into this league should study footage on Jimmy Butler," Spoelstra said.

The Lakers closed out the series in Game 6. But Butler's heroics showed fans in Miami that the Heat were a true contender once again.

Jimmy Butler's two triple-doubles in the 2020 NBA Finals kept Miami in the series against the favored Los Angeles Lakers.

TIMELINE

1987

The NBA Board of Governors votes unanimously to give Miami an expansion team.

1988

The Heat lose the first 17 games in franchise history before finally winning on December 14.

1992

The Heat make their first playoff appearance but lose to the Chicago Bulls 3–0 in the opening round.

1995

Pat Riley leaves the New York Knicks to become coach and president of the Heat.

1997

The Heat win their first playoff series, defeating the Orlando Magic 3–2 in the first round.

2000

The Heat open American Airlines Arena with a 111–103 victory over the Magic on January 2.

2003

The Heat select Dwyane Wade with the fifth overall pick in the NBA Draft.

2004

Wade hits a jumper with one second left in his first playoff game to defeat the New Orleans Hornets. Miami wins the series in seven games to advance to the second round for the first time since 2000.

2006

The Heat defeat the Dallas Mavericks 4–2 in the NBA Finals to win their first championship. Wade averages 34.7 points per game and wins series MVP.

2010

The Heat sign LeBron James and Chris Bosh. James announces his decision on an hour-long televised special.

2012

The Heat defeat the Oklahoma City Thunder 4–1 to win the NBA title.

2013

The Heat win a second straight NBA title, defeating San Antonio 4–3. Ray Allen's three-pointer with seconds remaining in Game 6 saves Miami from series defeat.

2017

Erik Spoelstra becomes the all-time winningest coach in team history, surpassing Pat Riley's previous record of 454.

2020

Led by star guard Jimmy Butler, the Heat reach the NBA Finals before falling to the Los Angeles Lakers in six games. Butler posts triple-doubles in both Miami wins in the Finals.

FRANCHISE HISTORY
Miami Heat (1988–)

NBA CHAMPIONSHIPS
2006, 2012, 2013

KEY PLAYERS
Bam Adebayo (2017–)
Chris Bosh (2010–16)
Jimmy Butler (2019–)
Tim Hardaway (1996–2001)
Tyler Herro (2019–)
LeBron James (2010–14)
Kyle Lowry (2021–)
Alonzo Mourning (1995–2002,
    2005–08)
Shaquille O'Neal (2004–08)
Glen Rice (1989–95)
Dwyane Wade (2003–16,
    2017–19)

KEY COACHES
Pat Riley (1995–2003, 2005–08)
Erik Spoelstra (2008–)

HOME ARENAS
Miami Arena (1988–99)
FTX Arena (2000–)
    Formerly known as:
    American Airlines Arena
    (1999–2021)

TRIVIA

LOGO CONTEST

Mark Henderson and Richard Lyons created the Heat logo in 1986. They put their entry in a design contest set up by the team and took 34 percent of the vote. The team still uses the original logo design.

FRANCHISE FIRST

Guard Rory Sparrow recorded the Heat's first triple-double on April 18, 1989. He had 24 points, 10 assists, and 10 rebounds against the Dallas Mavericks.

LENDING A HAND

The Chicago Bulls played an exhibition game in Miami as a fundraiser following the devastation of Hurricane Andrew in 1992. Michael Jordan and the Bulls won the October 19 game 111–94. The game raised more than $500,000 to help the area rebuild.

DAN THE MAN

In 2005 the Heat honored a Miami athlete who never set foot on a professional basketball court. Dan Marino was a Hall of Fame quarterback for the Miami Dolphins of the National Football League from 1983 to 1999. The Heat donated money to charity in Marino's name. The team also hung a banner with his No. 13 at American Airlines Arena in a special 2005 ceremony. The number was not retired, however, and is still worn by Heat players.

GLOSSARY

clutch
An important or pressure-packed situation; a player who often succeeds in important or pressure-packed situations.

draft
A system that allows teams to acquire new players coming into a league.

elimination
Knocking a team out of the playoffs.

expansion
The addition of new teams to increase the size of a league.

overtime
An extra period of play when the score is tied after regulation.

rookie
A professional athlete in his or her first year of competition.

timeout
A stoppage in game play that is called by one of the teams or players.

triple-double
Accumulating 10 or more of three certain statistics in a game.

veteran
A player who has played for many years.

BOOKS

Flynn, Brendan. *The NBA Encyclopedia for Kids*. Minneapolis, MN: Abdo Publishing, 2022.

Mahoney, Brian. *GOATs of Basketball*. Minneapolis, MN: Abdo Publishing, 2022.

Ybarra, Andres. *Great Basketball Debates*. Minneapolis, MN: Abdo Publishing, 2019.

ONLINE RESOURCES

To learn more about the Miami Heat, please visit **abdobooklinks.com** or scan this QR code. These links are routinely monitored and updated to provide the most current information available.

ABOUT THE AUTHOR

Tom Glave learned to write about sports at the University of Missouri. He has written about sports for newspapers in New Jersey, Missouri, Arkansas, and Texas. He has also written several books about sports. He looks forward to teaching his four children about all sports.